you read? It's best ...

them ii ... us order

1. **Pig** and the Talking Poo

2. **Pig** and the Fancy Pants

3. **Pig** and the Long Fart

4. **Pig** plays Cupid

5. **Pig** gets the Black Death (nearly)

6. **Pig** Saves the Day

7. **Pig** and the Ice-cream Cake

8. **Pig** Skives off School

9. **Pig** is a Blue Baboon's Bottom

10. Super**Pig**!

11. **Pig** and the Baldy Cat

12. **Pig** Leaves Home (for a bit)

PIG Leaves Home (for a bit)
by Barbara Catchpole
Illustrated by metaphrog

Published by Ransom Publishing Ltd.
Radley House, 8 St. Cross Road, Winchester, Hampshire
SO23 9HX, UK
www.ransom.co.uk

ISBN   978 178127 613 6
First published in 2013

Copyright © 2013 Ransom Publishing Ltd.
Illustrations copyright © 2013 metaphrog

A CIP catalogue record of this book is available from the British Library.

Leaves Home

(for a bit)

Barbara Catchpole

Illustrated by metaphrog

Ransom

Gran wins at bingo

It's been a big week here! Loads happening!

Guess what? Gran won at bingo!

Gran goes to bingo at the Tropicana Bingo Hall - the one with the statues of palm trees by the door.

It's next to the Day Centre, so when it's chucking-out time there, all the wrinklies go on to the bingo.

TROPICANA BINGO HALL

DAY CENTRE

Gran uses a special lucky bingo pen. It only does circles and it glows in the dark, in case there is a sudden power cut and some old person tries to steal your card.

Gran has a special lucky bingo baseball cap, too.

6

It has 'In it to win it' on the front.

She goes there with the Bingo Gang: Mary and
Daisy. They sound like lovely old ladies in flowery
dresses don't they?
They aren't! They
are terrifying.
Mary has a wart
on her nose
and yellow teeth
(she has at least
three).

Gran says Mary keeps a baby alligator in her
bath. Daisy only wears black leather with metal
studs.

Mary and Daisy both have sticks, but they don't need them to walk – they just use them as weapons.

They're like something out of Roald Dahl.

Mum won't let either of them in the house – not after Daisy stole our toaster.

Santa tried to go to
bingo with Gran
one week. Mary
hid his walking
stick and tripped
him up, and Daisy put
six sugars in his tea.

They don't like men.

When they are at bingo - watch out! It's
Terror at the Tropicana. (That would make a
great movie. Except it would be about bingo.)

Anyway, this week Gran won two hundred
pounds. There was a little bit of a row with

9

Daisy, who said Gran had stolen her numbers or something, but Gran can look after herself.

Gran's dead kind because she told Kim he was a good boy and he could take his guitar off eBay. She would pay for Suki to learn to walk.

Kim hugged her, and then he hugged his guitar, and then he hugged her again, until she fell off her walking frame and lay on the floor with her legs in the air.

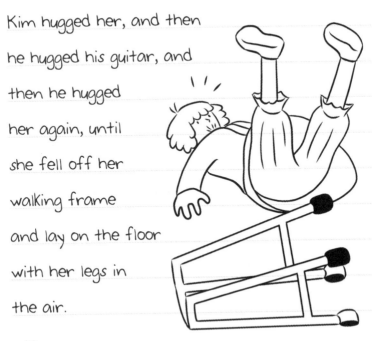

Then he had to pick her up and make her a cup of tea.

And Gran also bought Vampire Baby a baby walker. It's dead good – a bit like a space ship on wheels!

He whizzes round the kitchen in it. He pedals like mad, gets up some real speed, then lifts his feet up and crashes into the wall, shouting:

'Wheeeeeeeeeeeee!'

That's what I think he says, anyway. He's made a massive hole in the wall, next to the freezer.

You have to jump out of his way, because he rams your ankles and laughs. Suki said we could play 'Gran pin bowling', using Gran on her frame as the pins and the baby walker as the ball.

Mum said:

'A bit of gratitude wouldn't come amiss from you, my girl!'

But Suki didn't care.

Suki practises her walk (for being a supermod-el)

in the kitchen, too. So when Vampire Baby's in his walker she has to keep one eye out for him going at 70 mph at knee level.

It's fun to watch. Suki has to walk leaning right back, with one arm out and sort of jerking her hips forward. She has to hold her head up, too. That's the best time for Vampire Baby to strike – when she can't look down.

Her knees are getting very bruised. Suki looks like a big stick insect (with blue knees).

Tiffany came round and did some walking, too.

She was wearing a plastic silver crown she got for Christmas.

Tiffany wants to be a supermod-el as well.

14

(Why can't she walk at home, I want to know. Is there something special about our kitchen that makes you walk like a supermod-el?)

So everything was OK and we were all kind of happy.

Then Mum said to me:

'Pig, come into the other room. I need to talk to you.'

Then everything wasn't OK.

The talk

My mum is never nervous. She just doesn't do

'nervous'. If she had to meet the Queen, she'd just grin and say:

'Hiya, how's it going? Did you see 'Eastenders' last week? How are your kids doing?

'Baked beans are on offer down Tesco's — you should nip out from the Palace and stock up!'

16

There's nothing my mum can't do. If she wants to, that is. Some things she just won't do. Like go on a diet, or throw away left-over chips.

She's got pretty strong ideas about exercise as well. That's something else she won't do.

She was nervous this time, though. She had put on lipstick to talk to me.

17

What on earth was happening? I hope she didn't expect me to put on lipstick just to listen to her.

'You like Bob, don't you, Pig?'

Bob was OK. He just hung around with Mum a lot and ate our biscuits. I didn't need him – we were OK without him. The big thing was – Dad would come back soon and Bob would have to push off.

'Bob and I care a lot about each other. We were thinking, I might ask your dad for a divorce.'

It was funny. I didn't think anything at all. I just felt angry.

Mum was talking, but I wasn't listening. Her mouth moved, but only 'Bob, bob, bob' came out. Like a goldfish.

Then she said:

'You need a man about the house, Pig.'

I did need a man about the house, she was right. But not just any old man. Or any old Bob. I needed my Dad.

I got up and walked out without speaking and
without looking at her.

I heard her say quietly to herself:

'That went well.'

Monday

The weather girl said 'sunny
spells'. It rained all the
way to school. It tipped
down.

The Pits is down a bit of a dip, so it floods
easily. Sure enough, there were ponds in the
playground.

All the boys jumped in the puddles next to the girls and then said:

'Sorry!'

I absolutely soaked Kelsey Davis.

First lesson was a supply teacher because our ICT teacher had to take his lizard (called Iggy) to the vet. We were supposed to be looking up diseases that lizards can get (Sir loves Iggy).

21

Instead I found out where my dad lives in Spain. It was right on the beach.

I hate sand. It gets everywhere (and I mean everywhere). We've still got some sand that stuck to us when we went to Southend, and that was more than a year ago. Mum said you could tell it was Southend sand because it stuck to the baby's South End for weeks.

I looked up where the airport was and where my dad was. I printed it off. (You're not supposed to, but

the supply teacher bloke didn't know that.
Nobody tells supply teachers anything.) I told
him I was researching Spanish lizard diseases.

Tuesday

The weather girl said 'spells of
sunny weather'. It snowed a
bit on the way to school.
Everybody lies.

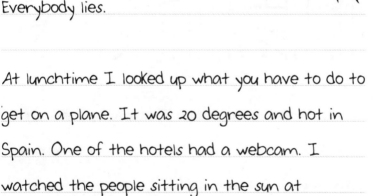

At lunchtime I looked up what you have to do to
get on a plane. It was 20 degrees and hot in
Spain. One of the hotels had a webcam. I
watched the people sitting in the sun at
lunchtime in the library. (That is, they were

23

sitting in the sun at the hotel. I was sitting in

the library at lunchtime, with snow outside.)

The librarian tried to get Tiffany to take out a

book. She asked if they had any on supermod-els

with lots of pictures. Tiffany doesn't do words.

24

Wednesday

Weather girl: nice and clear.

I couldn't see what the

weather was like today.

It was too foggy.

More kids come to school when it's foggy. The

attendance bloke says they wander in by

mistake.

25

Twenty-one degrees in Spain. I don't have a passport.

I took my mum's passport out of her drawer. (I did it with my eyes shut, because it's her underwear drawer - her 'drawers' drawer.)

It wasn't easy to find her passport because:

    a)   I had my eyes shut, and

    b)   she is a Big Panty Woman. The passport was under big-panty attack.

I put my new trainers in my backpack.

Thursday

Weather girl: mild and
spring-like. Bloomin' freezing
today. I put my finger
against the window in my bedroom to write my
name, and it got stuck to the glass. And I'm
sure the Spice Girls on my duvet had turned
blue.

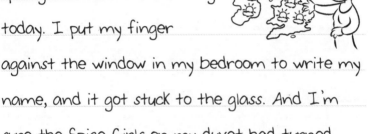

I gave Harry some extra bedding and the
inside of a toilet roll to eat.
I told him my plan and he
gave me a thumbs-up.

27

It was a good sign. He knows all about running away. He's great at it.

My phone's working great now, so I texted my dad that I was coming to live with him.

Tomorrow was the older kids' School Trip to the airport. I was going to go with them – but I was not coming back! Mwahahaha!

The great escape

I texted Raj and told him that I felt sick. He texted back that I probably had appendicitis.

I got on the coach with the other kids. The

teacher counted our heads, but I hid under my coat at the back when she checked numbers.

Ollie Gosnall fed me Haribo during the journey. I had to keep up my strength, after all.

Zoe Zwing kept jabbing me with a compass and laughing because I couldn't get her back.

When we got to the airport, I just walked in with the other kids. I put my hood up so nobody saw me. We walked in and I ran.

Then – whoaaaa! It was so huge! The airport was ginormous and there were so many people.

CHECK-IN DESKS

DEPARTURES

They were all rushing about and talking different languages.

It was really exciting. I just sat and watched for a bit.

The planes were enormous and I knew it was just air that held them up. I never understood that. Is it because people fart all the time and farts are lighter than air?

'Farts on a Plane': another great movie! (It would be a whodunnit! Ha ha.)

The plan

I was going to take Harry with me at first, but then I thought about it.

It would be difficult enough getting on a plane myself. What would I put him in? They haven't made a prison that can hold him.

We brought him back from the pet shop in a cardboard box. We don't have it any more because he ate it before we got to the end of Canal Street.

Harry would only escape on the plane. Then he would chew through some wire and the plane would plummet to the ground, injuring us all like in 'Grey's Anatomy' (Season 8). 'Hamsters on a Plane' - it would be a great film!

Anyway, I had a plan. I was going to wait for a big family or a school trip, and go with them to the plane. I would just wave Mum's passport and the guy would let me go through. Easy!

When I was near the planes, I would find the right one. It would probably have 'Spain Plane' written on the side, or maybe a number on the front - like a bus.

I would text Dad when I got to Spain.

I would be on the beach by tea-time (with an ice-cream with a little umbrella in it and chocolate sauce - no cherries, thank you, Dad, because they're fruit. I don't eat fruit).

The plan — the splash! bit

The plan went a bit wrong though. All that Haribo made me feel a bit funny. I went to the loo. (A huge, mega-load of toilets. It was hard to choose which one to go in.)

I was just checking how it flushed, because it had a button thing, and somehow I dropped Mum's passport down the toilet.

I just forgot it was in my back pocket. (No, it was before I did anything, thank you for asking!)

I tell you, the covers on those passports really don't stand up well to being down the toilet. You would think they would make them a bit better. I dried it a bit under the hand dryer, but it was still all wrinkly and pink.

The plan — still no luck

I waited for ages, but I couldn't see any big groups of people. I saw my own school group leave. Ollie Gosnall waved at me and pretended to be a monkey behind the teacher's back. Zoe Zwing made a rude sign.

Stranded

My phone pinged and I got a text. It was Dad.
Perhaps he could phone the airport and get me
a proper ticket!

I didn't know what to
do. I went outside
to watch the
planes take off
and land for a while.

I didn't cry - it's just so windy at those
airports - the dust gets in your eyes. I was
stranded. How would I get home?

I went back in, lay across a couple of those
plastic seats and went to sleep. When I woke

37

up it was dark. It wasn't night-time though. I think it was just the two huge security guys leaning over me and blocking out the light.

The white room

They held me by my arms and took me to a white room.

There were two hard chairs in the room. I sat

on one chair and a large lady in uniform stood at the door, guarding it.

Me:

'Am I under arrest?'

Uniform Lady:

[silence]

Me:

'Are you going to search me?'

(I was a bit worried about the damp passport
- perhaps you could go to prison for dropping a
British passport down the toilet, even if you
didn't flush.

Also, I was worried I might have to take my
trousers off. I had Bart Simpson underwear
on.)

Uniform Lady:

[more silence]

Me:

'Are you going to torture me?'

Uniform Lady:

'I might if you don't shut up!'

Me:

[silence]

Uniform Lady:

'I'll get you a coke if you tell me your

mum's phone number.'

Me:

[more silence]

I mean, who wants to be tortured?

Uniform Lady got tired after a while, so she had a little sit down and a doze in the other chair.

Mum to the rescue!

'Let go of me! Get off! Madam! Madam! Please! Ouch!'

'Get your hands off me! That hurt! Ooof! Help!'

'Ooof! Aargh! You mad old bat!'

Large Uniform Lady and I rushed out into the corridor. All my family were there, trying to get to me.

The shouting was coming from the Customs Officers.

Mum was struggling and being held by six officers. Suki was hitting out with her handbag. Gran and Santa were waving their walking sticks. Kim was holding Vampire Baby under one arm. He had his other hand over his eyes.

My mum shouted:

'Let him go, you bullies! I'll fight every one of you!'

The Customs Officers looked very afraid.

It's OK again

They wrestled Mum into the room and Uniform Lady brought her a cup of tea. Mum was breathing hard and her lipstick was all over her face, but she was grinning from ear to ear.

'I was so scared, Pig! I didn't know where you were! That Ollie boy told a teacher. It was the worst day of

45

my life! You're OK! You are OK, aren't you? I love you so much, you bloomin' nutter! So much! We thought you had been kidnapped!'

I tried to think what idiot kidnapper would try to get money out of my family. They watch too much television. I suppose the kidnapper could get left-over chips, instead of money.

If he was quick.

The school had texted Mum because I hadn't turned up. Who knew?

'Where's Bob?'

'He drove the minibus. He paid for it all.'

They had all come in a minibus, like when we went to the seaside!

Mum said they had argued all the way. Then Kim wanted to sing 'She's coming round the mountain' and they all shouted, 'Shut up!' at him. That made them feel better.

Mum asked if they were going to arrest us. Uniform Lady went and asked and came back and said:

'No, they are glad to see the back of you.'

Home

We drove home with everyone talking at once.

Bob drove through a McDonald's Drive Thru and bought me everything I asked for.

As soon as I was back, I went to tell Harry I was home, but he was out. Mum thinks he might be stuck in the Hoover pipe again.

48

Mum got hold of me and hugged me tight, as if she would never let me go. She kept laughing and telling me she loved me 'bucket-loads'. I had to ask her to stop because I was suffocating.

'We might be able take you to see your dad next year, Pig. We could save up.'

We?

I looked around the kitchen. The freezer door

was covered in school stuff. There was a huge packet of nappies on the table. Gran's walking frame and the baby walker had lots of wet washing drying on them.

Mum had left Harry's cage door open so he could get back in. I could see what was left of a gas bill in there.

50

I said:

'I'm not sure I want to go anymore.'

I was so happy I was home.

All of a sudden I knew, no matter what, home was just where I wanted to be.

Mum said:

'Oh, Pig!'

and she hugged me so hard it hurt.

How many of **PIG**'s books have you read?

About the author

Barbara Catchpole was a teacher for thirty years and enjoyed every minute. She has three sons of her own who were always perfectly behaved and never gave her a second of worry.

Barbara also tells lies.

52